Beast Quest®

TEKNOS
THE OCEAN CRAWLER

BY ADAM BLADE

ORCHARD

With special thanks to Tabitha Jones

www.beastquest.co.uk

ORCHARD BOOKS

First published in Great Britain in 2021 by The Watts Publishing Group

1 3 5 7 9 10 8 6 4 2

Text © Beast Quest Limited 2021
Cover and inside illustrations by Steve Sims
© Beast Quest Limited 2021

Beast Quest is a registered trademark of Beast Quest Limited
Series created by Beast Quest Limited, London

The moral rights of the author and illustrator have been asserted.

A CIP catalogue record for this book is available from the British Library.

ISBN 978 1 40836 214 3

Printed in Great Britain

The paper and board used in this book are made from wood from responsible sources

Orchard Books
An imprint of Hachette Children's Group
Part of The Watts Publishing Group Limited
Carmelite House, 50 Victoria Embankment, London EC4Y 0DZ

An Hachette UK Company
www.hachette.co.uk
www.hachettechildrens.co.uk

Welcome to the world of Beast Quest!

Tom was once an ordinary village boy, until he travelled to the City, met King Hugo and discovered his destiny. Now he is the Master of the Beasts, sworn to defend Avantia and its people against Evil. Tom draws on the might of the magical Golden Armour, and is protected by powerful tokens granted to him by the Good Beasts of Avantia. Together with his loyal companion Elenna, Tom is always ready to visit new lands and tackle the enemies of the realm.

While there's blood in his veins, Tom will never give up the Quest...

TO
AVANTIA

PORT
CALM

THE LOST
CITY OF VIGA

WOODS
WITHOUT
END

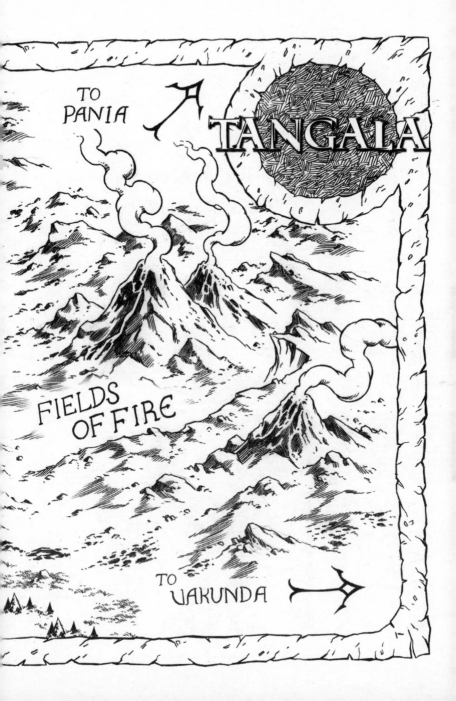

There are special gold coins to collect in this book. You will earn one coin for every chapter you read.

Find out what to do with your coins at the end of the book.

CONTENTS

It is always said that Tangala has no Beasts. That, I'm pleased to say, is not quite true. There are Beasts here – terrifying ones – but they are sleeping. I will awaken them. I will fill them with rage and evil. And I will set them loose on the people of this kingdom.

Vakunda was my prison, but now I'm free. They thought I was dead. They were wrong.

I have lived for five hundred years. I have vanquished any who stood in my path. No puny Avantian boy will stop me now. My Beasts will ravage and destroy Tangala and I will stand over the ruins, ruler of all.

Zargon

AN UNINVITED GUEST

Tom popped a fourth jam tart into his mouth and sat back in his chair, watching as couples dressed in their finest clothes swirled across the dancefloor. Shafts of afternoon sunlight streamed through the throne-room windows, making the silverware on the banqueting tables

shine. Music and laughter filled the
air. Tom let out a satisfied sigh.

From her seat beside him, Elenna
leaned in close, smiling. "Rotu looks
like he's having a great time," she
said. On the dance floor, the prince
bent low over his partner's hand,

then swept her into a spin.

"He deserves it after everything he's been through," Tom said. "I'm glad nobody's expecting us to dance, though."

Elenna laughed. "I still ache all over from our last Quest!"

Tom and Elenna had recently helped Queen Aroha rescue Prince Rotu from the Evil Wizard Zargon, in the magical kingdom of Vakunda. Now they were guests of honour at a banquet held to celebrate Rotu's safe return to Tangala. Thankfully, they had been spared from wearing formal court dress, though their boots and weapons were polished to a high shine.

Elenna lifted her glass of spiced apple juice and clinked it against Tom's. "Here's to happy endings!" she said. Tom started to raise his own glass but noticed an armoured Tangalan guard striding towards the queen. The tall, muscular warrior was frowning, her riding boots spattered with mud as if she'd just arrived. Tom's heart sank and he let out a groan.

"This doesn't look like good news," he said. "We'd better find out what's going on."

Elenna nodded. As they stood, Daltec, dressed in a silver-trimmed wizard's cloak, also rose from his seat. He too was watching the guard, his brows knitted with worry. Tom, Elenna and Daltec all reached the queen's table together.

"Your Majesty," the guard said, bowing low, "I have just returned from Vakunda. Our troops have searched every corner of the kingdom, and of Zargon's ruined palace. There was no trace of a body."

Aroha lifted troubled eyes to Tom, Elenna and Daltec. "It is as we feared," she said. "Zargon must somehow have escaped."

Coils of dread twisted like snakes in Tom's gut as he thought of how close he and the others had come to death the last time they faced the wizard. Zargon was one of the deadliest enemies Tom had ever met. The Evil Wizard had been imprisoned in Vakunda for five hundred years, and Tom knew he would stop at nothing to wreak revenge on Tangala.

"So much for our happy ending!" Elenna said. She turned to Daltec.

"Is there any way you can use your magic to trace Zargon?"

Daltec shook his head. "If I had something that belonged to him, I might be able to. But unfortunately, we have nothing."

"Well, wherever he is," Tom vowed, "while there's blood in my veins I'll—"

A chorus of yells and the scrape of chairs being pushed back cut off his words. The music faltered, and Tom heard shouts coming from outside. He and Elenna raced to the nearest window. Far below, guards were hurrying about in the courtyard as purple smoke billowed through a pair of wrought iron gates at the far end. Beyond the gates, the doors to an ornate stone building hung open, with more of the purple smoke pouring out from inside.

Behind Tom, Aroha gasped. "The crypt!"

"Stand back!" Tom cried, then, calling on the magical flight of Arcta's eagle feather, he vaulted on to the windowsill. Tom lifted his shield above his head and leapt...

Clouds of acrid purple smoke parted around Tom as he swooped through the air towards the crypt, angling his shield to guide his flight. He swooped low, narrowly missing the spikes that topped the iron gates, and landed in a run.

Fumes stung his eyes and caught in his throat as he sped into the half-darkness of the mausoleum and down a flight of steep stone steps.

At the bottom, he found himself in a long, dark corridor. Most of the smoke had cleared, but eerie purple light flickered from a side chamber, casting ghastly shadows across the walls.

Tom took a deep breath, then lifted his sword and leapt into the chamber. Zargon stood at the back of the room. Purple light crackled from his gloved fingers to run like forked lightning over the smashed remains of four broken tombs. A pile of weapons lay at the wizard's feet – a sword, a mace, a spear and an axe.

"Stop this sacrilege!" Tom cried.

Zargon's eyes narrowed. "It's too late for that, boy!" The wizard's thin lips spread in an evil grin and he jabbed a finger at Tom, sending out more jets of purple energy. Huge chunks of stone rose from

the remains of the tombs and shot towards Tom.

Tom dived aside. Broken slabs sped past his head, smashing against the wall behind him. Zargon snarled, and with a flick of his fingers, sent another barrage of rubble hurtling across the room. Tom lifted his shield. *THUD!* A massive hunk of stone slammed into it, throwing him back against the wall. Winded, his arm numb to the elbow, Tom somehow kept his shield raised.

"I'll bury you alive!" Zargon hissed. More lumps of stone flew through the air. But instead of hitting Tom they clattered down, one on top of each other at his feet, quickly forming a wall around him, piling higher, sealing him in.

Tom called on the magical strength of his breastplate and slammed his shield into the wall. Pain jolted up his arm, but the wall held fast. More stones piled on top, blocking his view… Sick panic rose in Tom's throat. *I'm trapped!*

THE WEAPONS OF THE ANCIENTS

"Stop!" Elenna cried, her voice cutting through the crackle of magic and the thud of stone. Zargon let out a furious howl. The purple light fizzled out, and in the sudden darkness, Tom kicked again at his rock prison. This time, it collapsed with a crash.

Two Tangalan guards burst into the room behind Elenna, their torches casting a flickering light through

the chamber. Tom saw Zargon yanking angrily at his cloak. It was pinned to the wall at his back by one of Elenna's arrows. She already had another fitted to her bow, and quickly aimed it at the wizard's chest as he managed to tug his cloak free.

Zargon cast an icy glare around the room, then with a wave of his hand he vanished in a flash of light, taking the weapons at his feet with him.

Elenna hurried towards Tom. "Are you all right?" she asked. "You're bleeding!"

Tom wiped at a stinging patch on his cheek. "Just a scratch," he said. "If you hadn't broken Zargon's spell before he finished, I'd be walled into my own burial chamber by now." Tom and Elenna frowned at the four broken tombs. In the wavering light from the soldiers' torches, Tom could just make out the shrouded remains inside.

"How could Zargon do something so horrible?" Elenna asked. "And why?"

"I'm not sure," Tom said. "But he took four weapons with him when he vanished."

"We must tell Aroha at once," Elenna said. "Whatever Zargon wants with the weapons of the dead, it can't be good."

Tom and Elenna arrived back in the throne room to find guards ushering the last few guests from their tables. Aroha paced backwards and forwards but stopped as she saw Tom and Elenna. From the haunted look in her eyes, Tom knew she had been told what had happened.

"Come with me," Aroha said, leading them into her study – a small, bright room just off the main chamber. Daltec was already there, seated near the fire. He looked up as they entered, his face etched with worry.

"So, Zargon is up to his old tricks," Daltec said.

Elenna sighed. "I knew it was too

much to hope that we'd seen the last of him. What do you think he's planning?"

Aroha lifted her hand towards a long, faded tapestry that hung behind her desk. "The answer to that lies in the past," she said.

Tom had noticed the tapestry before, but never really taken in the detail. He ran his eyes along the needlework now, making out four armoured warriors, each fighting a mighty Beast many times his or her own size. Each warrior wielded a different weapon – an axe, a sword, a spear and a mace.

"Those are the weapons Zargon took!" Tom said, pointing.

Aroha nodded. "They were crafted by his own hand, many centuries ago," she said. "They were made in a time when Tangala was looking for a new Master or Mistress of the Beasts. Four young warriors, two male and two female, set out on a Quest to compete for the role. Each was sent to a different corner of the kingdom to defeat a Beast that had been laying waste to the regions there. Zargon, a royal wizard at the time, furnished each knight with a magical weapon that would remove the evil from the Beast's heart and lay the creature to rest."

At the bottom of the tapestry, below the fighting warriors, Tom could see four great stone tombs.

"I see it didn't end well," he said.

Aroha sighed. "No. Though each brave warrior defeated their opponent, all four were mortally wounded... They died on the same fateful day. They were named Masters and Mistresses of the Beasts in recognition of their sacrifice and buried here at the palace along with their weapons."

"And now, even their graves have been desecrated!" Tom said, fresh horror washing over him. "But what does Zargon want with their weapons?"

"I think I can answer that," Daltec said. "As the four weapons were used to lay Beasts to rest, they can also be used to raise them, restoring their Evil."

Aroha nodded. "And from what we know of Zargon, we can be sure that's exactly what he intends to do."

"Then the whole kingdom is at risk!" Tom said. "He could be anywhere by now, and we have no way of finding him!"

"Don't be so sure," Elenna said, smiling grimly. She held a small scrap of fabric out towards Daltec. "Would this be enough to work your magic?"

Zargon's cloak! Tom realised. *Good thinking, Elenna!*

Daltec took the fabric, running his thumb over it. "It's worth a try."

The young wizard muttered an

incantation and waved a hand
towards the tapestry. The needlework
blurred. Tom blinked to find the
picture replaced by a view of high,
white cliffs above a bay as calm as a
millpond. A figure with long dark hair

and a wizard's cloak stood at the top of the cliff looking out over the sea. *Zargon!*

"I recognise that place," Aroha said. "It's on the far western shore of Tangala, near a harbour town called Port Calm."

Daltec's eyes refocussed and he waved his hand over the tapestry. It shimmered and the vision disappeared, becoming the faded embroidery once more.

"Can you transport us there?" Tom asked his friend.

Daltec gnawed his lip. "I should be able to get you close," he said.

"Get us as near as you can, and I'll have no trouble finding the cliff,"

Aroha said. "I know every part of Tangala."

"Your Majesty," Daltec said, frowning. "I think it may be better if you stay here. Word will quickly spread about what has happened. Your people will be uneasy, and your presence will reassure them."

Aroha clenched her fists in frustration. "I have no patience for waiting around. I want to fight this wizard, to bring him to account…"

"You can trust Elenna and me to ensure Zargon is brought to justice," Tom said.

The queen shook her head. "But—"

"There's a chance he could return here, to Pania," said Elenna. "If he does, you're the only one who can protect your city."

The queen sighed. "You're right. Go then, Tom and Elenna, with my blessing."

Tom turned to Elenna. "Ready?" he asked.

She slung her bow over her shoulder, and Tom felt grateful again that they were wearing their ordinary clothes. "Always!" she said.

Daltec held out the scrap of cloak. "Touch this and brace yourselves," he told them. Tom and Elenna each held a corner of the fabric. As Daltec started to chant once more, the walls of Aroha's study lurched into a spin.

Whoa! Tom almost staggered. He

planted his feet wide as the room swirled faster and faster, round and around...then, like a candle being snuffed, everything went dark.

Tom's ears popped. Cold blackness pressed in on him. *Water!* It surrounded Tom, filling his nostrils, his mouth. He clamped his teeth shut just in time to stop himself drowning. He blinked, straining to see in the murky gloom. *Elenna?* He couldn't see her. Tom's lungs throbbed with lack of air. Panic knifed through his gut. *I can't drown! I haven't even started my Quest!*

A COLD WELCOME

Trying to ignore the burning pressure in his lungs, Tom forced himself to stay calm, and to think. Which way was up? He breathed out a stream of bubbles and kicked after them.

The gloom gradually brightened, and soon Tom could make out the surface shimmering far above him. *Desperately far…* His lungs shuddered for breath and his blood thumped loudly in his ears, but he pushed himself on towards the surface. Finally, just as he thought his lungs might burst, he broke through into daylight. Gasping and panting, Tom looked again for Elenna. *Where is she?* He couldn't see anything through the murky water. He swallowed his rising panic. *She has to be close!*

Tom was about to duck back under the surface to find his friend, when Elenna shot from the water at his side, heaving a huge, ragged breath. After she had recovered, she pointed towards a rocky shoreline not far off.

"I think that was where Daltec was aiming," she said.

They both began to kick towards the land, and in no time were dragging themselves, shivering and sodden, out on to a shingle beach.

"I'll definitely be glad when we're back in Avantia, and Daltec's magic works like it's supposed to," Tom said. "But first we've a wizard to catch."

Further along the curving coastline, Tom could see what looked like a bustling town. Dinghies and rowing boats bobbed in the choppy grey water alongside a quay. The dry docks of a small shipyard jutted into the ocean, overshadowed by a pair of tall wooden cranes. *Port Calm, Aroha called it.* Using the enhanced eyesight of his magical golden helmet, Tom saw children sitting on a promenade that ran along the seafront, fishing for crabs, and men working on the skeleton of a ship in one of the docks.

"I can't see any sign that Zargon has woken a Beast," he told Elenna.

"Let's hope we're in time to stop him," Elenna said.

Not far from the beach, they found a muddy coastal road, pitted with cartwheel ruts. They followed it towards the town, and before long they could hear the hammer and clink of wood and metalwork, along with laughter and jovial voices.

As they passed the first cottages on the outskirts of the town, Tom saw a young woman hanging out washing. He smiled and lifted a hand, but the woman's eyes darted to the sword at his belt, then widened in alarm.

"Don't be afraid—" Tom started, but before he could finish, she tucked her bag of pegs into her apron and hurried inside, slamming the door.

Tom and Elenna walked further into town, getting similar reactions everywhere they went. Children ran

from their path, casting anxious
backward glances. Groups of
chatting locals eyed them sidelong,
then dispersed, shutting their doors
firmly before Tom and Elenna could
say hello, let alone ask if they had
seen anything suspicious.

"Should we head to the seafront?"
Elenna said. "An inn might be more
welcoming."

It certainly couldn't be less so...
Tom thought. It didn't take long to
reach the busy promenade, backed
by workshops and taverns. But even
here, weatherworn men shot them
dark looks, then shuffled away,
brows furrowed. Only a pair of older
women sitting outside a tavern held
their ground. They were chatting as
they repaired a lobster creel. Just as
Tom thought he might finally be able
to ask about Zargon, both women
got up and ducked into the tavern.

This is hopeless! Tom thought. But
then the tavern door banged open

and one of the women reappeared. She was followed by a huge, muscled man with a greying mane of reddish hair and thick red beard to match. He swaggered forward, shirtsleeves rolled up to the elbow, revealing thick and tattooed forearms. His huge, calloused hands looked strong enough to crush Tom's skull.

Tom stood straight and smiled. "Hello," he said, extending a hand. The big man ignored it and leaned in close, peering into Tom's face with fierce blue eyes. His skin was so deeply lined and reddened by the wind it was hard to tell his age.

The man stepped back. "I'm Azrael," he said, his gaze flicking

between Tom and Elenna. "But you
two can call me 'Chief'. Now tell me,
what's a pair of soggy brats doing
carrying weapons into my town? You
should know only the queen's guard

is permitted to carry blades."

Tom's anger flared but he did his best not to let it show. "We come from Queen Aroha," he said. "We—"

The man cut Tom off with a harsh bark of laughter. "Pull the other one!" he said. "What would Her Majesty want with whelps like you?"

Tom took a deep breath. "We're on the trail of an Evil Wizard. You may have seen him. He has dark hair and a long black cloak. He's very dangerous. We must find him before he resurrects four Beasts from Tangala's past."

The chief's colour deepened, and he jabbed a huge finger at Tom. "Look!" he growled. "We may be simple fishing folk, but we're not stupid!"

Four more burly men shouldered their way out of the tavern and lined up behind him.

"There's been no Beasts in this

part of Tangala for longer than I can remember," the man went on. "And wizards in black cloaks? Poppycock. Put down your weapons. You're getting locked up until you learn respect enough to tell the truth!"

From the corner of his eye, Tom saw Elenna's hand flinch towards her bow. More men slunk from the tavern, and soon a dozen scowling giants had gathered behind their leader. Tom's shoulders slumped. He knew they couldn't fight their way free. *Not without hurting someone.*

He caught Elenna's eye and shook his head. Then, going against his every instinct, he unbuckled his sword, and laid it on the ground.

CAPTIVE

Dust swam in the dim rays of light
filtering through the floorboards
above Tom and Elenna. Sitting against
the cellar wall with his hands tied
behind him, Tom could just make out
stacked barrels and piles of fishing
net. He shifted his weight to ease the
pain in his arms, but it was no use.

Elenna wriggled, trying to pull

her wrists free of their bonds. She grunted in frustration. "Why didn't you let me put up a fight?" she asked. "While we're trapped down here, Zargon could be doing anything!"

Tom tried to shrug but couldn't. "We might have escaped," he said, "but someone would have been injured – another innocent victim of Zargon. No…I'd rather win the villagers' trust. That way, we can find out what they know."

"Well, we can't do *that* right now, either!" Elenna said. She started tugging at her bonds again, but soon let out a growl and gave up.

Suddenly, a door creaked open at the top of the stairs above

them. Light streamed through. Tom
stiffened, expecting to see Azrael;
but instead, a small, dark-haired girl
appeared. She cast a furtive glance
behind her and quickly ducked inside,
shutting the door.

"Are you here to stop the creepy man
that's been hanging around by the
cliffs?" the girl asked. She didn't look
older than seven, but her voice was
steady and bold.

Tom's pulse quickened. "Who do
you mean?" The girl hurried down the
steps to peer more closely at Tom and
Elenna. Whatever she saw seemed to
satisfy her. She nodded and perched
on a barrel.

"I keep seeing this weird old man

on the beach," she said. "He's got a long staff or something. And he wears a long black cloak, just like you said. He's no fisherman. I told Father, but he didn't believe me. No one does. He said, 'Clara, stop making up stories.' But just because I'm little, doesn't mean I'm stupid." The girl tossed her head proudly, and Tom smiled, suddenly seeing a resemblance between her and the town's chief, Azrael. *He must be her father!*

"I believe you," Elenna said. "The man you describe sounds like the person we're tracking. He's up to no good, and we mean to stop him!"

"That's what I thought!" the girl said, nodding again, her serious face lighting up with relief. "So, I watched where my father put your weapons. He's in town now, talking with the other elders about what to do with you – but they always take ages to decide anything!" She whipped a hand from behind her back, revealing a short, curved knife. She grinned, then quickly sawed through Tom and Elenna's bonds. Putting a finger to her lips, Clara led them upstairs into the kitchen. The light outside was fading now, and a low fire burned in the hearth. Clara took a key from a drawer and opened a tall cupboard. Inside, Tom spotted his sword and Elenna's bow among the mops and brooms. He grinned.

"He may not realise it yet," Elenna
told the girl, "but you've done your
father proud! Now, can you tell us
where you last saw the old man?"

"I'll do better than that," Clara

said, puffing out her chest. "I'll show you. I know every route through town! I'll take you a back way, so you won't be seen."

"Perfect!" Tom said. "Let's go!"

They emerged from the house to find the streets shrouded in murky shadow. Clara led them quickly on tiptoe, keeping close to the narrow doorways of closed workshops and silent warehouses.

From the distant seafront, Tom heard the occasional burst of talking and laughter as a tavern door opened, mingled with the constant hushing of the waves. Suddenly, Clara signalled for them to stay silent. She crouched low, leading them below a carpenter's window where the torchlight spilling into the street and the sound of hammering warned of someone inside working late.

As they rounded a corner, Tom heard muffled voices and footsteps

from ahead; but again, Clara was ready. She dipped into a narrow alley, gesturing for Tom and Elenna to follow. In the gloom, they all waited, barely breathing as three men strode past.

"—a pair of foreign children carrying weapons, apparently," one of the men was saying. "No wonder Azrael doesn't know what to do with them."

"One of them was going on about wizards and Beasts too, I heard," another added. All three laughed.

"Beasts? In our town? That's ridiculous! Although, do you remember that huge fish I caught the other day? That was a monster and no mistake. Maybe that's what the lad saw." The men all guffawed. They were still laughing as they strode out of sight.

I only hope they never face a real Beast! Tom thought.

Eventually, Clara led Tom and Elenna past one final long, low building and out into the open. The setting sun shone red and gold over a curved stretch of still water, lighting it up like molten iron in a crucible. A high cliff rose above the bay's narrow beach.

"That's where I saw him earlier today," Clara said, pointing at the beach.

Tom gazed about at the dazzling

water, the high, craggy cliff. Then he lifted his eyes, and gasped. A figure stood at the top, silhouetted against the fiery sky, cloak whipping in the breeze. *Zargon!* But it wasn't a staff he was holding – it was a spear. In the eerie quiet, Tom could hear him chanting strange, guttural words.

"He's casting a spell!" Tom cried. "Clara – find your father and warn him. I have to stop Zargon before he raises a Beast!"

There was only one way to approach. If he ran straight at Zargon, the wizard would see him coming. But if he climbed up the rockface instead, he might be able to sneak up. He set off along the beach, hidden under the cliffs, and then began to climb. There were plenty of handholds and ledges to set his feet in, so he made quick work of the ascent. When he reached the top, he peered over the edge. The wizard had lifted the spear and blue light crackled from the tip. Tom scrambled the final part of the climb, then laid one hand ready on the hilt of his sword.

"Stop this, villain!" he cried.

When Zargon saw Tom, his eyes flashed with hatred and his lips curled into a cruel sneer. He flung his hand outwards, fingers splayed as he shot a jet of sizzling light from his palm. The magical energy slammed into Tom's chest, flinging him backwards off the cliff.

The shield slowed his fall, but Tom landed back in the shallows with a *splat* that knocked his breath away.

He struggled up, blinking and coughing saltwater away, and looked up to see Zargon surrounded by crackling blue light, the spear in his hand glowing. The wizard drew back his arm, aiming the weapon. Tom lifted his shield, but then realised Zargon wasn't looking at him. With an exultant cry, the wizard sent the spear sailing over Tom's head, far out into the water. It sank into the depths.

Why has he done that? He's lost the

weapon for ever, surely...

Silence filled the bay as ripples spread outwards from where it had struck, leaving the sea glassy and unnaturally still in their wake.

Tom threw an uneasy glance at Elenna.

Blub... Blub... Two huge bubbles rose to the surface and burst. A moment later, with a sound like a geyser blowing, a great patch of water started to boil and foam. Filled with dread, Tom turned to see Zargon, outlined by the fiery light of the setting sun, throw back his head and laugh.

THE OCEAN CRAWLER

"Elenna! Cover me!" Tom shouted as he staggered from the shallows. "I'm going to try and reach Zargon again."

Elenna lifted her bow, aimed an arrow at the cackling wizard and let it fly. Calling on the power of his golden boots, Tom leapt again, following the arrow's path. Water streamed from his clothes as he shot upwards, over the cliff edge and landed in a run.

Sidestepping Elenna's arrow, Zargon lifted a hand. The wizard's fingers sizzled with magical energy, but Tom didn't slow. He cannoned into Zargon, throwing him off balance. They went down together. Tom landed on top, grabbed a fistful of the wizard's cloak then aimed a punch at his face.

Zargon snatched Tom's wrist from the air before he could land the blow.

"I told you, you're too late!" Zargon spat through clenched teeth, then he clutched Tom's throat with his free hand and squeezed.

No. I'm. Not! Eyes bulging, gasping for breath, Tom gripped the wizard's outstretched arm firmly, calling on the magical strength of his

breastplate and rolling towards the cliff-edge. Over and over they went; Zargon struggling to get free, Tom holding fast.

For a heartbeat, they teetered at the edge, locked together. Stones tumbled down the rockface beneath them...

Then, *whoosh!* Tom's stomach flipped. They plummeted through the air, Zargon's cloak billowing around them. *We'll both die!* Tom thought. But at the last possible moment, the wizard conjured a glowing ball of golden energy that ballooned into a giant bubble of light to cushion their fall. Zargon released his grip, and they both

rolled off. The golden glow faded.
Lifting his sword, Tom flung himself
at the wizard. But Zargon clicked
his fingers, conjuring a shield of
silver light. When Tom tried to hack
through, pain jolted up his arm and
he almost dropped his blade.

From behind the forcefield of light,
Zargon grinned, then pointed a
single finger at Tom. Purple energy
crackled at the wizard's fingertip.
"I'll fry your brains for meddling
with my plans!" he snarled.

"Think you're quicker than my
arrows?" Elenna said, stepping from
the shadow of the cliff to stand
behind the sorcerer, an arrow nocked
and ready.

As Zargon spun to face Elenna, his forcefield vanished. Relief surging through his body, Tom took the chance Elenna had created. He lunged, hooked his foot around the wizard's ankles and scooped his legs

out from under him.

Zargon hit the ground with an "Oof!" then rolled on to his back. Tom planted a boot on the wizard's chest. Elenna still had an arrow ready.

In the sudden quiet, Zargon glared up at them, furious. Then Tom heard a rushing, roaring sound coming from the sea – quiet at first, but quickly getting louder.

"Whatever evil magic you have unleashed, undo it now, or you die!" Tom demanded.

Zargon grinned, his dark eyes filled with spite. "I can't," he said. "Teknos the Ocean Crawler has risen, and all in his path shall perish!" Then, with a flick of his fingers as if he were shooing a fly, Zargon vanished. Tom stumbled forwards, thrown off balance.

"Tom!" Elenna cried. Tom turned to see something rising through the boiling water of the ocean, huge and craggy, almost like an island. The mound rose higher, and a massive scaled head broke through the waves. Dark, slanting eyes scanned the beach, and a gnarled but powerful-looking beak snapped open, letting out a bellowing roar. *A giant turtle!* Tom realised. In the creature's terrible cry, he could hear rage and confusion, fury and anguish. Vast flippers the size of

rowing boats pushed through the
water, dragging the colossal Beast
towards the shore. A bulbous
spiked tail rose behind Teknos,

then crashed back down, sending up a spray of water. The creature's flippers churned the rising waves as it forged onwards, sending them higher, so they built into a tremendous swell, rolling towards the beach.

Glancing back at the cliffs, Tom felt his heart clench. *When those waves hit, we'll be pummelled against the rocks! We'll never survive!* There was only one thing for it.

"Elenna! We have to get to higher ground!"

RAMPAGE

Tom and Elenna pounded over the sand towards the cliff face. The roar of the ocean was so loud, Tom expected to be swept away by a wave at any moment. Glancing back, he gasped. The dark wall of water towered over him, curling into a high, foaming peak. Tom considered leaping to the clifftop.

But I can't leave Elenna. We'll climb together! They both threw themselves at the rockface and scrambled upwards. Sharp stone grazed Tom's hands and knees, and his wet boots slipped, making his heart leap into his mouth – but he managed to hang on and keep going.

Elenna climbed like a spider, quickly passing Tom, swarming up the almost vertical cliff.

"Hurry!" she called back. With the thunder of water in his ears, Tom wondered if he'd made a mistake. But he couldn't jump now. He pulled himself onwards, faster than ever.

The wave struck the cliff and

surged upwards. Water slammed
into Tom's body, pummelling him
with icy fists. As quickly as it hit,

the wave retreated, sucking at Tom, threatening to pull him to his death as he clung on with his fingertips.

Another wave crashed against him. Then another. He could hardly keep hold of the stone with his numb fingers. Finally, the water receded. Dripping wet and chilled to the bone, Tom looked up to see that Elenna had climbed high enough to stay almost dry, but her face was pale as she gazed out over the ocean.

"Tom!" she cried. "The village!" Tom turned to see the huge bulk of Teknos cutting through the dark, choppy water towards the glittering lights of the harbour.

"We'd better hurry," Tom told

Elenna, seeing how fast Teknos moved.

They both scrambled down the cliff face, jumping on to the beach as soon as they were close enough, then raced over the wet sand. The sun had set, and as they approached the village, they could see boats and taverns silhouetted black against the twilit sky. Orange points of light showed where torches burned behind windows, but while Tom watched, some were blotted out by the curved mound of Teknos's vast body as the Beast heaved himself ashore.

Screams and the crash of splintering wood filled the air. Tom and Elenna sped along the coastline and leapt up on to the harbour's wooden promenade to find Teknos destroying the dry docks with his massive, club-like forelimbs while villagers ran for their lives.

A half-finished sailing ship blocked the Beast's path, but instead of going around the boat, Teknos ploughed straight ahead, powerful beak snapping through wood and massive flippers batting shattered planks aside. Reaching the promenade, Teknos didn't slow. His limbs thrashed like the sails of a windmill. Tom's heart lurched when he spotted a pale face peeking from under the hull of an upturned boat, right in the Beast's path. *Clara!*

Elenna had already spotted the girl and was sprinting her way.

"I'll distract the Beast!" Tom called after her, reaching for the red jewel in his belt. *Teknos! These people mean you no harm!*

Teknos powered on, heedless. Fear jolted through Tom as Elenna reached Clara right at the moment Teknos lifted his massive foot to

crush the small boat.

Stop! Tom told the Beast, putting all the force he could muster into the command. Teknos froze. His vast head swivelled towards Tom, a spark of understanding in his eye.

Shadowed beneath the Beast's raised
foot, Elenna grabbed Clara by the
hand and pulled her into the shelter
of a doorway.

With his eyes still on Tom, the Beast
lowered his massive limb, smashing
the empty boat to pieces without even
seeming to notice.

*Leave this town and return to the
sea*, Tom told Teknos.

So tired... The Beast's groggy voice
spoke in Tom's mind. *Head hurts...
Body hurts... Must sleep...*

Tom felt a flicker of hope. He was
getting through to the Beast!

But suddenly, Teknos's voice
changed, becoming a low, angry
rumble. *Tiny people woke Teknos!*

Smash them! Crush them! Make them pay!

The Beast lumbered off again, heaving his mighty body towards a tavern. The villagers peering from the building's windows and doors screamed with terror. A few men made a run for it.

Stop! Tom told the Beast once more. *You don't need to do this!* This time, Teknos shook his giant head as if to get rid of Tom's voice from his mind, then let out a bellow of rage.

Back at Tom's side, Elenna lifted her bow and aimed for the Beast's eye.

"Wait!" Tom told her. "Teknos isn't all bad. There's still goodness in his heart. We must defeat him without killing him."

Elenna turned wide eyes on Tom. "How?" she asked. "He's like a battering ram. Those people are all going to be killed!"

As if to prove her words, Teknos rammed his scaled head into the tavern's front wall. With a mighty crash, beams snapped, and the walls slanted. Howls of terror echoed from inside.

"Cover me as best as you can!" Tom told Elenna. Brandishing his sword, he raced forwards, reaching Teknos just as the giant turtle shoved his beak through a huge hole where the tavern's door had been.

I am Master of the Beasts! Tom told Teknos through the power of his red jewel. *I can help you, if you'll stop and listen.* Teknos whirled around to face Tom.

Must attack! the Beast bellowed in Tom's mind. He snapped for his throat with his sharp beak.

Tom leapt back just in time, running his eyes over the colossal turtle. *He must have a weakness, surely…*

But as Tom looked for a chink in the Beast's scaly armour, Teknos whipped around, his clubbed tail swinging. Tom lifted his shield, but the tail's bulbous tip hit him like a huge mace, flinging him through the

air. Tom slammed into the wrecked
wall of the tavern and slid to the
ground. He tried to stand but the
grating agony in his ribs snatched
his breath away and he slumped
back down.

Glancing up, he saw Teknos haul himself away over the ruins of the promenade. Tom let out a sigh of relief. But then a red-haired man stepped out of a building to stand in front of Teknos, brandishing a club. *Azrael!* The huge turtle let out a growl and heaved himself up on to his back legs to tower over the village chief.

Tom's blood ran cold as he realised Teknos was about to flatten his victim.

NO WEAK SPOT

Clamping a hand over his injured
ribs and grimacing with pain, Tom
forced himself to his feet and called
on the magical speed of his golden
leg armour. He hurtled towards
Azrael, leaping the broken planks of
the walkway. Teknos, balanced tall
on his hindlimbs, stood higher than
the rooftops. Still wielding his club,

Azrael looked as small as a child.

Tom reached him in two mighty
bounds, threw his arms around
the huge man's chest, and yanked
him off the walkway. They landed
heavily together on the sand amid
the broken remains of boats. Pain
spiked again under Tom's ribs as
Teknos's body crashed down on to
the promenade above them.

Azrael stood and brushed himself
off, his face still ashen and his eyes
wide. "I owe you my thanks, lad," he
said, clapping Tom on the shoulder.

"You're welcome," Tom said, doing
his best not to wince at the pain
in his ribs. "But you can't defeat a
Beast with a club. Get your people

to safety, and leave the fighting to us."

The big man looked doubtful for a moment, but then glanced at Tom's sword and shield, and then at Elenna, who was aiming an arrow at Teknos as the huge Beast heaved himself up. Azrael turned back to Tom and tipped him a respectful nod, before vaulting back up on to the damaged walkway.

"Abandon your homes and follow me!" Azrael bellowed as he strode away into the town. A few people emerged from behind doorways and under boats to follow their chief.

Tom hurried to Elenna's side as she fired again at the Beast, the arrow ricocheting harmlessly off Teknos's shell. The giant turtle snapped at a shop roof, ripping away a hunk of thatch, then brought his huge forelimbs down on to the wall, crashing right through it.

"This is hopeless," Elenna told Tom. "He's not going to stop until he's destroyed the whole town."

"Our weapons aren't even slowing him," Tom said. "But maybe we can trap him somehow!" Gazing around the twilit harbour, Tom could just make out the shape of a huge fishing net down on the beach, hanging on a stand to dry.

"This way!" he said, beckoning to Elenna as he broke into a run.

With the Beast busy pulverising the remains of the shop beneath his giant feet, Tom and Elenna made a dash for the net. It was heavy and unwieldy but, each gripping a corner, they managed to haul it from the rack, up the beach and towards the seafront.

Teknos paused in his destruction to gaze about, looking for a target. Tom and Elenna took the chance to skirt round behind the Beast and creep up close. Keeping well out of range of his massive tail, they both lifted the net as high as they could.

"Now!" Tom cried. He and Elenna hurled the net over the Beast's back. It caught on the lip of his

shell. Teknos's head instantly jerked
around and he let out a roar of fury.
Tom and Elenna grabbed the

trailing end of the net.

"Hold him!" Tom told Elenna. But the words sounded foolish in his own ears. The Beast was so big!

Teknos shook himself, trying to throw the net free. Tom's teeth clashed together as he was jerked about, but he didn't let his grip weaken.

The Beast roared again, then started to move. Even using the magical strength of his golden breastplate, Tom staggered forwards. Elenna was yanked clear off her feet. Together, they were dragged behind the Beast as he tramped up a sloping street and into the town. Tom pulled back

with every sinew of his strength
and dug in his heels, trying to slow
the Beast while looking desperately
for something to fasten the net to.
But the Beast trudged on as if Tom
and Elenna weighed nothing at all.
*He's too strong even for my Golden
Armour!* Tom thought, feeling as
small and powerless as one of the
barnacles on Teknos's shell.

With a sudden bellow of rage, the
Beast shook himself again. Tom's
bones rattled as he was tossed from
side to side. Unable to shrug off the
net, Teknos turned his head.

CHOMP! The Beast's razor-sharp
beak snipped through dozens of
thick strands at a time. *CHOMP!*

The severed net slid free. Tom
and Elenna tumbled backwards.
Scrambling to his feet, Tom called

to the Beast with his mind. *Leave this village! Leave these people, and sleep once more!*

Teknos turned towards him, his eyes flashing with fury. *TINY PEOPLE WILL DIE! YOU WILL DIE FIRST!* he roared in Tom's mind. Tom swallowed, his throat suddenly dry. He knew the Beast's terrible beak would be able to crunch through bone almost as easily as net.

"Head for the harbour!" Tom told Elenna. "If we lure him into the open, we'll have more space to fight!" But even as he said the words, he felt suddenly heavy with dread. *How can we possibly defeat a Beast with no weak spots?*

TURNING THE TABLES

Tom and Elenna raced back the way they had come, the Beast's footsteps thundering behind them, his bellowing cry ringing out into the night. As they reached the dusky harbour, Elenna stopped suddenly, and pointed at the one remaining crane standing beside the smashed dry docks. A chain with a hook for lifting heavy timbers hung from the top of the winch, attached to a pulley at the bottom.

Elenna flashed Tom a grin. "There is one sure way to render a turtle defenceless," she said. "Even a huge

one like Teknos!"

"Of course!" Tom said, suddenly smiling too, although he knew the plan would be difficult and dangerous. "You get ready with the pulley, and I'll lure him over!"

Tom stood tall on the beach and waved both arms.

Over here! he called to the Beast through the red jewel. *If you want to crush me, now's your chance, brute!* Teknos appeared from between two buildings, lifted his head and roared. Then he stomped towards Tom. Glancing towards the base of the crane, Tom saw Elenna already in place, with her hands on the pulley handle.

Teknos lurched through the promenade and down on to the beach, throwing up shingle and sand as he hauled himself towards Tom. With the Beast's furious gaze fixed on him, Tom circled back

towards Elenna, stopping just under the hook.

Opening his huge, sharp beak, Teknos lunged suddenly. Calling on the power of his golden boots, Tom leapt up over the Beast's snapping

jaws, and on to Teknos's shell.

I will kill you! You will die! Teknos arched his neck, trying to reach Tom. His beak snapped on the empty air right in front of Tom's face.

His neck isn't long enough! But then the Beast started to buck. Tom's stomach lurched as his feet slipped. Letting his sword and shield fall, he dropped to a crouch, gripping the edge of Teknos's shell with his fingers and toes as the creature shook and reared, trying to throw him free.

Looking up, Tom could see the hook right above the lip of Teknos's shell. Gripping with one hand, he reached for it, and found it with his fingertips. Teknos bucked again, and Tom just managed to fasten the hook into place before he tumbled.

He hit the sand awkwardly and rolled, scrambling to his feet to see Teknos come for him, beak wide open, and eyes flashing with fury. Tom's heart shot into his mouth... But just before the massive beak closed on his throat, Teknos jerked to a halt. Looking up, Tom saw the chain attached to the hook had pulled taut. *Phew!*

"Wind the pulley!" Tom called to Elenna. The chain started to rattle and clank. Teknos heaved against it, his head writhing from side to side.

"I could do with a hand!" Elenna called. Tom raced past the thrashing

creature to join Elenna at the
pulley, putting his hands on the
winch beside hers. With them both
heaving together, the handle started
to turn. Elenna grunted with effort.
Sweat dripped down Tom's face

and his arms burned, but Teknos was tipping upwards, rising until he stood high on his hind legs... With another heave on the pulley, the Beast tipped backwards slightly. Teknos roared with anger and fear as he teetered...then toppled!

The Beast landed on his back. His legs beat the air and his head whipped from side to side, but there was no way he could right himself. He was stuck. Tom and Elenna turned to each other and slapped hands in an exhausted high five.

STUCK! Teknos roared in Tom's mind. *CANNOT GET UP!* Tom's attention snapped back to the defenceless creature. Walking closer to Teknos's mighty upturned body, Tom found a point midway between the turtle's thrashing legs and leapt up on to his belly. With one hand on the red jewel in his belt, Tom placed the other, palm down, on Teknos's shell.

Hush now, Tom told the Beast. *Be calm. I don't want to leave you like this. I want to help.*

STUCK! Teknos roared again.

I know, Tom said. *I want to help, but you* must *stay calm…please.*

HELP! Teknos said, and Tom noticed his voice sounded less angry and more desperate now.

I know you're not Evil, Tom told the Beast. *I know you are just angry*

because someone woke you when
you were supposed to stay asleep.
But hurting people won't solve that.
If you promise not to harm anyone,
you can go back to the sea in peace.

For a long moment, Teknos didn't
say anything, but Tom could sense
the Beast's ancient mind working,
his anger fading. Even the shell
beneath Tom seemed to be changing,
becoming smoother. A marbled
pattern appeared, shining in the
moonlight. It was actually quite
beautiful.

Help! Teknos said again at last,
and now his voice sounded weary,
but calm. *Help, and I go.*

Tom leapt down from Teknos's

belly and ran to Elenna.

"We did it!" he told her. "Zargon's curse has been lifted, and Teknos is Good again."

"So I see," Elenna said, smiling as she gazed at the Beast, no longer encrusted with barnacles, but as smooth and polished as a beach pebble. And there was a gentleness in the creature's huge dark eyes that hadn't been there before. "But we still have a problem." Elenna said. "How are we going to turn him back over?"

Tom's heart sank. Then he heard a mighty cheer. He turned towards the harbour, to see a crowd of people had gathered, and in the moonlight, he could just make out Azrael at the front, with Clara at his side.

"The Beast is Good now!" Tom called to the townsfolk. "But he's stuck. We need to turn him over so he can get back out to sea where he belongs." No one moved. Tom heard a few mutters from the crowd, but not a single person stepped forwards. Except Clara. The small girl hopped down from the remains of the walkway and on to the beach. Tom and Elenna led her to stand beside the Beast.

"He's perfectly safe now," Tom told her. Clara nodded, and tentatively put out a hand to touch the creature's shell. Teknos blinked his dark, liquid eyes, acknowledging the touch, and Clara smiled.

"Come on, Father!" Clara called back to the crowd. "Everyone! He needs our help!"

Azrael walked slowly forwards, joined by tens, and then scores of the townsfolk. Together, they took position on one side of the Beast, and began to push him upwards. As they lifted him, others joined the effort, laying hands on Teknos's shell to force him higher. Finally, with much grunting and one massive joint shove, they rolled the Beast on to his front. As the townsfolk jumped and slid back on to the beach, a second cheer went up, and people hugged, clapping one another on the back.

Teknos took a long look at the cheering villagers, then swung his body around and crawled away across the sand towards the lapping tide. The moonlight glanced off his

shell as he forged into the waves.

Tom's heart felt full as he watched the Beast vanish under the peaceful sea. Elenna was smiling as she gazed after Teknos, and Tom noticed a misty look in her eyes. He put a hand on her shoulder.

"It's not often we get a real happy ending, is it?" Tom said. Then he spotted Azrael striding towards them from the gathered crowd. He and Elenna turned towards the village chief, hurriedly clearing their throats. The big man put out a hand to Tom.

"I'm sorry I didn't trust you," Azrael said. Tom shook his hand warmly, and Elenna did the same.

"I won't judge so quickly by appearances next time," the chief added.

"I understand," Tom said. "You were trying to protect your village. But now that evil has come to Tangala, we must all join together and fight!" Tom glanced inland over the dark cliffs, and the warm glow he'd been feeling vanished, leaving him suddenly chilled. Zargon was still out there, with the power to wake three more Beasts. *But wherever he next appears, while there's blood in my veins, I'll be ready!*

THE END

1

CONGRATULATIONS, YOU HAVE COMPLETED THIS QUEST!

At the end of each chapter you were awarded a special gold coin.
The QUEST in this book was worth an amazing 8 coins.

Look at the Beast Quest totem picture opposite to see how far you've come in your journey to become

MASTER OF THE BEASTS.

The more books you read, the more coins you will collect!

Do you want your own
Beast Quest Totem?
1. Cut out and collect the coin below
2. Go to the Beast Quest website
3. Download and print out your totem
4. Add your coin to the totem

www.beastquest.co.uk

8

READ THE BOOKS, COLLECT THE COINS!
EARN COINS FOR EVERY CHAPTER YOU READ!

550+ COINS
MASTER OF THE BEASTS

550+
515
480
445
410
395
380
365
350
320
290
260
230
217
206
191
180
146
112
78
44
30
19
8

410 COINS
HERO →

350 COINS
WARRIOR

230 COINS
KNIGHT →

180 COINS
SQUIRE

44 COINS
PAGE →

8 COINS
APPRENTICE

READ ALL THE BOOKS IN SERIES 26:
THE FOUR MASTERS!

*Don't miss the next
exciting Beast Quest
book: MALLIX THE
SILENT STALKER!*

*Read on for a sneak
peek...*

GHOST WARRIOR

Tom and Elenna stood side by side,
high on a clifftop at the western
shore of Tangala, gazing out over the
moonlit sea. Tom felt gritty-eyed and
bone tired after their recent battle
with Teknos, a giant turtle-Beast. He
took a deep breath, relishing the cool

breeze on his skin.

Gentle waves rolled on to the shadowy beach far below – the water calm again, now that Teknos had been returned to his resting place beneath the ocean. But still, dread gnawed at Tom's gut. Though he and Elenna had managed to save the nearby fishing village of Port Calm from Teknos's furious rampage, their Quest had only just begun.

Zargon, a powerful Evil Wizard, had stolen four ancient, magical weapons from the tombs beneath Queen Aroha's palace – each capable of awakening a mighty Beast. Crazed with revenge, Zargon would stop at nothing until he had brought the kingdom of Tangala to its knees.

"Not while there's blood in my veins!" Tom vowed under his breath.

The problem was, they had no way of knowing where to head next. No map, no clues. Zargon could be awakening another Beast at that very moment, and they'd be powerless to prevent him.

A sudden gust of icy wind slammed into Tom from behind, almost pitching him and Elenna over the cliff. He caught his balance and grabbed Elenna's sleeve, pulling her back from the edge. They both turned and froze. The grass rippled silver in the moonlight and the dusky shadows swirled.

"What's that?" Elenna asked, her voice tight with fear. In the darkness, a huge, pale shape coalesced before them. Tom gasped as he made out a woman standing tall on a chariot pulled by two gleaming white horses, their coats dappled with shifting purples and greys. The woman's hair and the manes of the horses eddied gently around them as if underwater, and Tom realised he could see the stars through their ghostly forms. The woman's face was pale, like marble, and shimmered with a radiant light, but her coal-dark eyes seemed to bore into Tom's very soul. Tom gripped the hilt of his sword firmly as the woman raised a hand, palm forwards.

"I mean you no harm," she said, in a deep voice that penetrated the wind. In her other hand, she held a spear – an exact duplicate of the one Zargon had thrown into the ocean to awaken Teknos.

"Who are you?" Tom murmured – although in his heart, he knew she had to be the warrior who had first laid the turtle-Beast to rest, then perished, more than four hundred years ago.

"I am Celesta," the woman said. "I congratulate you both on your victory. Teknos sleeps once more, and for that, I am eternally grateful. But now a terrible Evil arises in the

North. Even as we speak, a Beast is stirring deep in the Forest of Shadows – Mallix. Unless you can stop him, innocent lives will be lost."

Tom had no idea where the forest was, but there was sudden fire in his heart. "Show us the way," he said.

"It is many days' travel," Celesta said. "My horses will guide you." The two white stallions tossed their silver manes and raked the ground as if eager to leave at once. Celesta stepped gracefully from her chariot and gestured for Tom and Elenna to take her place.

Tom turned to Elenna. Her eyes shone wide in the moonlight, but she nodded firmly. They straightened their backs and strode towards the ghostly vehicle. Tom stepped gingerly on to the translucent platform, half expecting his foot to go straight through; but though he could see the grass below, it felt firm. As Elenna climbed aboard, Tom took the reins, inhaling sharply at the icy burn of the leather in his hands.

"Thank you," he said to Celesta. "And farewell. We will not let you down." The ghostly warrior dipped her head, her dark eyes holding Tom's to the last as her form melted into the night.

Tom turned to the horses – a perfectly matched pair, powerfully muscled and taller than any living steeds. He gave the cold reins a tug.

The two horses surged towards the cliff edge so fast Tom's stomach flipped. "Whoa!" He pulled on the reins, straining his muscles, trying to slow the phantom creatures, but they careered on, picking up more speed. Tom's heart shot into his mouth as they leapt out into the darkness. Elenna gasped, her knuckles white on the chariot's rim.

We're going to fall!

But instead of plummeting, the horses soared upwards, carrying them swiftly into the night sky. A fierce wind battered against Tom and made Elenna's short hair whip about her face. The impossible speed tore at

Tom's stomach. But his fear quickly gave way to breathless elation as the stallions surged onwards, heading north. The landscape sped past in a dark blur below, villages no more than clusters of lights and rivers gleaming like silver snakes. Tom's heart filled with hope. As if in response, one of the stallions lifted his head and let out a joyful whinny.

Read
MALLIX THE SILENT STALKER
to find out what happens next!

ULTIMATE HEROES

Find out more about
the NEW mobile game at
www.beast-quest.com

Meet three new heroes with the power to tame the Beasts!